POETRY TO PLACATE DECEPTION;
VERACITY!

POETRY TO PLACATE DECEPTION;
VERACITY!

SHELDON D. STOVALL

Author of Internationally Celebrated,
Back to the Beginning: The Journey

Unlike folded hands across one's chest, truth never dies, nor does it rest. Within the covers of this book, the truth is told; the whole truth, and nothing but the truth!

Introduction by Stuart Abrams
Foreword by Gary Nichols

Copyright © 2021 by Sheldon D. Stovall

Published by S. D. Stovall Productions sstovall1213@gmail.com

Metoyer-Roy Printing, Ltd.
2400 Central Parkway, Suite D
Houston, TX 77092

All rights reserved. No part of this book may be copied, reproduced, or transmitted in any form by any means, manual, electronic or mechanical, including but not limited to photocopying, scanning, recording, or by any information storage and retrieval system without written consent and permission by the publisher and or author. Request for reproduction or related information should be addressed to:

S. D. Stovall Publishing, e-mail address sstovall1213@gmail.com

For information about special discounts for bulk purchases, please contact Mr. Stovall at 281-536-3771 or sstovall1213@gmail.com. If you would like the author to make a live appearance at your event as a speaker or panelist, to do a book signing, or a live poetry reading, please also contact S. D. Stovall Publishing, e-mail address sstovall1213@gmail.com.

Manufactured in the United States of America

Cover Photo: Cheryl L. Stovall

Cover Design: The Author & Sheldon W. L. Stovall

Editing: Sheldon W. L. Stovall

Biography Photo: Priscilla Graham

Also by Author and Poet
Sheldon D. Stovall

Published Works

Back to the Beginning: The Journey
Select YMCA Poems

Future Works

Poetry Because
Stoetry
Humorous Nicknames and How They Got'em

CONTENTS

Table of Contents	I
Latin Quote on Truth	V
Dedication	VI
Introduction	VII
Foreword	IX
Foreword Cont.	X
Preface	XI
Spring	XIII
Time	XIV
Self Portrait	XV
A Father's Day Poem…	XVI
Jesus Standing on My Feet	XVII
ONE	
Poetry to Placate Deception	2
The Undisputed Truth	3
No Time to Waste	5
Time Better Spent	7
Wisdom and Knowledge	8

CONTENTS cont.

TWO

	Do the Right Thing	10
	The Story of the Newcomers	12
	I Will Get Up	14
	The Truth Is	15
	The Joy of My Life	16
	A Prayer for Ricky	17
	Butchie	18
	Aunt Mae	20
	Griffen	22

THREE

	In Time, Truth Will Prevail	24
	I Saw the Light	25
	Just 48 Hours	26
	The Real Olympics (1976)	27
	Still Here	29
	Haiku	30

FOUR

	It is Us	32
	These Formative Years	33
	Pick-up Sticks	34
	Marbles	35

CONTENTS cont.

Pop Goes the Weasel	37
What a Meal, What a Meal	39
Chew the Peg	40

FIVE

Church Bells Ring	42
Not the Shaker but the Shook	43
Nothing to Show	44
Win, Place, or Show	45

SIX

I Got It Right	48
It's Spring	50
I Killed a Man	51
Just the Basics	52
I Could Not Catch Up with Life	53

SEVEN

I Am Privileged	56
Summer Days	57
Sunday Morning Prayer	59
Bedtime Baby Rhyme	60

CONTENTS cont.

EIGHT

I'm Tired of That Same Old Grind	62
Granny; 100 Years Old	63
The Black Poets' Legacy	65
To Rewrite History	67
Not Done Yet	68

NINE

A Place for All	70
Truth Never Dies	71
My Mind	72
The Parade	73

TEN

Blessings	76
My 1958 Olds	77
The Lie	78
Pilish	79

"Vincit omnia veritas"
(Truth conquers all things!)

Dedication

I dedicate this book to the four family members whose timeless poetry is shared in the preface: my father, Waymond J. Stovall Sr., my deceased brother, Waymond J. Stovall Jr. (Skip), my wife, Cheryl Stovall (Sugar), and my sister-in-law, Lander Rose Stovall. Thank you all for allowing me to share your work.

In memory of
Leslie Clifton Mitchell Jr.
May 7, 1949 - March 17, 2020

Introduction

Sheldon Stovall is a poet of tremendous talent, and a force of creative energy, unlike many have seen. His poetry reverberates in the heart, stirs the soul, and challenges the mind to aspire more profound levels of greatness.

His poetry has the ability to speak to real life situations and breathe new energy into those who have lost their way. His work is filled with humor, wisdom, vision; and it speaks to the trials and tribulations that God brought him through. It speaks to the substance of things hoped for and the evidence of things not seen.

Without question, his poetry will make you laugh, cry, think and have faith where there was once none. This is poetry that flows like a river and shines like the brightest day!

Stuart Abrams, Author; "More Than a Conqueror"

VIII

Foreword

Gary Nichols; Historian, Senior Vice President YMCA of Greater Houston, Retired

Sheldon Stovall:
Teacher, Scout Executive, Outreach Youth Specialist,
YMCA Executive in Ohio, then Texas,
Youth and Adult Achievers Recognition Program,
"Smooth Talkers" Middle School debate program,
Houston Texans YMCA Founding Executive,
Adjunct Professor with Springfield College,
And finally, Poet Laureate and Author.
Incomparable achievement all!

Throughout his long career in service
as a YMCA Professional Director and Vice President,
Sheldon Stovall has mastered the
principles of *The Power of One*:

An understanding of oneself:
"Wisdom begins with the desire to engage." (Natalie Hanson)

A passion for mission:

"A transcendent cause, something to live for outside of myself."

A commitment to mattering:

"Do not walk through life without leaving worthy evidence of your passage." (Pope John 23)

A legacy for those to come:

"The higher joy is not the light, it's the reflection. The greatest pleasure is not climbing up, it's handing down." (Bruce Feiler)

Sheldon Stovall lives all four principles, and on the pages which follow, he shares with us, once again, his mastery of the written word, through his inimitable poetic wisdom.

"No smell, no taste, no persona, no face.

Truth is the example we see,

The way we ought to be.

Poetry to placate deception. Veracity!"

Preface

I've been putting my thoughts on paper for a very long time; not always politically correct, but always with, what I call, poetic logic and license. When I told my Dad that I wanted to major in English and be a writer, he said I needed to do something that would feed a family. I tried to do both; gave 100% to my job, and wrote when I could. I always wanted to work with kids; from substitute teaching high school, right out of college, to Boy Scouts, to a Lifelong career working with youth and families with the YMCA.

As a very young kid, and even now, I always marveled over "old folks". Their life stories and experiences always fascinated and thrilled me. That's one of the reasons why Mr. Mease, my mentor was so special to me. I wanted what he had: faith, wisdom, knowledge, understanding, peace of mind, and truth!

I've had health issues for more than half of my life, but I've always felt blessed. I had the greatest role model on dealing with my medical condition from my Mother, Ossie Stovall, who suffered from poly-cystic kidney disease, as I do. I watched her go to work, go to dialysis, come home and cook, maintain a six-member household, and then do it all again the next day. She did this for over 15 years; never complained and always showed love and caring for others; the strongest faith of anyone I've ever known.

My Dad wrote poetry as far back as he can remember. I've included two of his poems in this opening: one of which he wrote at the age of thirteen. I guess my brother and I followed in our father's footsteps. Both of us began oral rhymes and rhythmic writing at an early age.

My immediate and extended family have often used poetic metaphor, rhyming prose, and lyrical parables to explain life's phenomena. As far back as I can remember my grandparents, great aunts and uncles shared their experiences in a way that transcended the common language; mythological poetry, if you will. This tradition has been passed down to my grandparents, parents, and sibling, thereby providing me with the impetus needed to be a vessel of the written and spoken word.

My talented father, brother, sister-in-law, and wife have all put-to-pen their natural aptitude and emotional style of expression, some of which I'll share here. What follows in this preamble is an example of their work, and the poetic talent that permeates within, and throughout, my family tree. This is the truth, as it has been revealed and passed down to me. Five poems. Four poets. Truly inspiring poetry.

Spring

Waymond J. Stovall Sr.

Now that Spring is here at last,
And all the cold winter days have past,
Let's watch nature take its place
Through all the gentle world of space.
Watch the trees as they turn green;
Watch the flowers. It's a beautiful scene.
I believe nature is really a friend,
For it's God's best gift to men.

Time

Waymond J. Stovall Sr.

The sun shines through the window with glow,
While I sit in the classroom, as time goes slow.
It goes so slow I often wonder why;
They say time waits for no one. It passes you by.
Sometimes time can be a friend to me,
And then again, an enemy.
I wish time would hurry up and score.
So it will be, "school's out", at quarter to four!

Self Portrait
Waymond J. Stovall Jr.

WHY DOES THIS MAN PRETEND TO BE
WHEN OTHERS SAY HE'S NOT
IS IT BECAUSE OF PETTY JEALOUSY
IS IT BECAUSE THEY CAN'T UNLOCK

A WRITER'S TALK IS HIS OWN TO MAKE
THAT NO ONE MUST TRY AND SCARE
FOR THESE ARE CHANCES HE MUST TAKE
TO GAIN RESPECT FROM THOSE WHO CARE

MY GOALS IN THE REALMS OF LIFE
CANNOT BE FOR MY FRIENDS TO SAY
FOR WITH TEDIOUS WORK AND MORAL STRIFE
I'LL MAKE IT TOMORROW PREPARING TODAY

A Father's Day Poem for My Husband

Cheryl "Sugar" Stovall

A noble man you are,

God fearing, giving

Honest and caring

You are the poet

And I must say

A pretty darn good one

Everybody knows it

This being my first poem,

You're thinking, it should be my last,

Just wanted you to know

In our two score years together

Life has been a Blast

A wonderful father, husband, and friend

Enjoy these special days

Forever, always,

To the end.

Jesus Standing on My Feet

Lander Virdure Stovall

Jesus standing on my feet,
And I on his, walking down the street.
Making sure I stay straight on the path
Until we meet.

Thank you, God, for my salvation,
And helping me keep my sanctification.
You sent your Holy Spirit and it's deep down inside.
Sitting on my soul so I don't lose my stride.

With a three-fold cord, your spirit ties my will, emotion, and weakness,
As it releases your love, joy, and meekness.

I want to shout the "good news" so heaven can hear
Of your goodness, grace, and mercy.
But I hear that still, small voice say, "I'm always close. I'm always near."

"Just listen with your heart. As long as you want me, we will never part.
Remember, I knew you long before your start;
I was here before your beginning, and I will be here when you depart."

Lord it is your face I seek, sometimes I can't hardly speak.
Will you give me a glimpse of heaven..just a little peek?
That's okay. I'll wait. It will be such a treat.

And He said, "I'll be at heaven's gate, just don't you be late."

ONE

"A dishonest person, when talking, is more than likely not telling the truth!" **Sheldon D. Stovall**

Poetry to Placate Deception; Veracity!

How much oppression can you take?
How much tolerance can you fake?
How many deceitful hands can you shake,
Before the lies, you can negate?

Truth can't be measured or weighed.
It can't be earned or payed,
Sold upright or laid; it just is!

Truth is what Satan rearranges.
Knowing Truth is the one constant that never changes.
It can't be cut, curved or bent.
Truth is Heaven sent!

Truth is light! And light is what we seek!
The quest is not for the weak,
But for the humble and the meek.

When you receive light, you can see the Truth.
Truth can dry up uncontrollable tears.
Truth can destroy the enemy,
And conquer fear.

No smell, no taste, no persona, no face.
Truth is the example we see;
The way we ought to be.

Poetry to placate deception; Veracity!

The Undisputed Truth

Thank you for the Miracle, I never doubted your word.

Because doubting you,

Would be the sign of a disbelieving fool;

Ridiculous and absurd.

You showed me what prayer and faith can do,

And through me, you proved that believing is true.

I know why old folks pray,

And why those who say

They don't believe

Run away.

It's the fear of the unknown;

The fear of things not seen;

And these folks not perceiving themselves

As truly spiritual beings.

But let me assure you, from a person who died

And saw the light;

Brought back to life.

As an example of your favor,

So that others can savor

The miracle that is,

That can be,

For all that believe.

The spirit is real.

Believing is factual, and life is a privilege,

Not a sacrilege.

Follow your dreams, and let your dreams follow you,

But keep the faith;

Believe. And the miracles that are in store,

That you pray for,

Will come true and be yours!

This is the divine covenant to you!

This is the promise;

The undisputed Truth!

No Time to Waste

It's not a crime,

But I'm wasting my time

Going in the wrong direction.

Make a correction.

I must save my brain,

And get off this train,

Before I go totally insane!

Jump the track;

Head back!

To a better place

And space;

No more time to waste.

I must prepare

To take a dare,

So that I can get there!

Get to a new destination

Without hesitation

Or any explanation.

Chart a new course;

Be a new me!

Let me envision and see

A new being.

May light be my compass and guide

To take me on my final ride.

My fate I will abide!

Now, unto the Most High unknown;

To the Crown and the Throne.

Time Better Spent

Don't come looking for trouble.

For if it's trouble,

You brought it here.

You're always in the middle of a confrontation;

Bullies spreading fear.

Slow your role

Before it takes its toll.

There's someone more ruthless than you.

There's always a bigger fool!

Ease up, back off, before

You become the laughing stock and a bore.

Don't dish out pain

Or make it rain

On someone else's parade.

Lift them up.

Make the embarrassment stop.

Don't cause the sore to fester.

Turn your harassment

Into a supportive gesture,

A kind word;

Time better spent.

Wisdom and Knowledge

There is a difference between

Knowledge and Wisdom.

The variances are that

Understandings are originated through life's personal experiences.

Knowledge is what you read, hear, and realize

From the occurrences and incidents of the lives of others.

Wisdom is what you've learned, absorbed, and acquired over time,

From living!

It is void of inexperience and ignorance.

So;

Keep learning.

Keep absorbing.

Keep discovering.

Keep living.

TWO

Fix your thoughts on what is true and good and right.

Philippians 4:8, ***The Living Bible***

Do the Right Thing

Most Animals, whether they be wild or domestic, are trainable. But only human beings are equipped with the ability to think, make decisions, and react at a high level. An elephant trainer begins to train this massive wild beast to stay in one place very early. When the young elephant is first weaned from its mother, he is chained to a stake. As he grows, he doesn't try to get away because he has been conditioned to think that he can't. In reality; the stake in the ground and attached chain can't hold this large super strong animal, but the elephant over time has been accustomed to staying put.

And so it is, with the domestic animal and man's best friend, the dog. You can place an electric collar around its neck synchronized with an electric fence around a perimeter. When the animal crosses the invisible fence equipped with an electric charge, it triggers the electric boundary and the dog receives a shock . It only takes a few passes before the dog is conditioned and knows not cross the line. If he does, he will suffer the consequences.

Humans have a moral fiber that generally conforms to a standard of righteous behavior. We have the ability to think and use the knowledge that we have been given to separate right from wrong. We are born with the capability to make decisions and behave accordingly.

This behavior is an intricate part of our values, our individual character, and it directs us, sometimes without conscience thought, on doing the right thing.

Morality is not what we do, so much as who we are. Who we are in turn, determines what we do. Our system of values and morals is so much a part of us that we cannot separate it from ourselves. It becomes the navigating system that directs and guides us, forcing us to do what's right.

Martin Luther King Jr. once stated, "Cowardice asks the question, 'Is it safe?' Expediency asks the question, 'Is it political?' Vanity asks the question 'Is it popular?' But conscience asks the question, 'Is it right?' And there comes a time when one must take a position that is neither safe, nor political, nor popular, but one must take it because one's conscience tells one that it is right."

As human beings, we know what is right and true. We can choose to follow the path of righteousness and truth, or we can ignore our gut and the invisible little birdie on our shoulder, and be ignorant to our conscience. We must use our God-given ability to think, make decisions, and act accordingly. We must always, as stated in the Title of Spike Lee's 1990 Oscar nominated movie, *"Do the right thing!"* .

(Parts of this piece are ideas read years ago in an essay from an unknown author.)

The Story of the Newcomers

The story is told about a young couple, known as the Newcomers, who, in search of a better life, migrated to the New Land from the Land of Old. The Blessed took the Newcomers in and helped them gain permanent residence among them. They gave the Newcomers housing, clothed them, and provided them with food. They trained them on the ways of the New Land, and provided them with work, so that they could live and prosper.

Over time a baby was born to the Newcomers. They raised her in this new environment teaching her some of the ancient ways of their ancestors and history of the Land of Old. They also made sure, with the help from the Blessed, that she was nurtured, given the best education; active socially, involved in the community, and exposed her to the culture of the New Land. She actively participated in all the wonderful programs of the Blessed and accepted every part of the experience. She grew into a young Newcomer and along with her parents, learned and enjoyed the ways of the New Land.

One day, the Blessed asked the young Newcomer to share at a New Land Blessed Festival. She would provide the opening for the day long festivities. During her opening she praised the Blessed and thanked them for accepting her and teaching her so many wonderful things.

She shared that it was so amazing that she could keep the spiritual beliefs of her ancestors in the Land of Old and be a young leader in the New Land. It was a true and sincere affirmation.

The next day, many of the Blessed talked with each other and were disturbed that the young Newcomer would mention the ways of the Land of Old. Others thought she should have never been picked to give the Festival's opening because she was an outsider; a Newcomer. The Blessed continued to talk among themselves and word got back to the young Newcomer that the Blessed disapproved of her message. The young Newcomer became distraught and withdrawn, and all that was learned by her was forever lost.

The family of Newcomers never associated with the Blessed again instead they sought out other Newcomers, and never again ventured outside the Newcomer circle.

I Will Get Up

I will get up!
I can't stay down.
Bad things happen, but I will get up.
I must rise above mendacity and hypocrisy.
I must reach a place where honesty
Out runs pretense and duplicity.
Where lies go to hell, and truth prevails.
I seek reciprocity, from what is,
To what can be; will be; must be!
I will rise above the lies.
I will get up!
I will get up!
I will stay up!

The Truth Is

The truth is!

Lyrics don't make a love song.
And rhyming lines don't make a romantic poem.

Commitment and caring bring people together.
But honesty keeps them united during stormy weather.

So, make the written words sing,
And love will be the results it brings.

It will feed the spirit and nourish the soul.
It will consume the script with stories untold.

The Joy of My Life

To my surprise,

She fell out of the sky,

And became the joy of my life.

My partner, my companion, my wife.

My encouragement to win the fight.

My confidante when I can't get it right.

A falling star, on the darkest night,

Illuminating my world, and eliminating my strife.

A Prayer for Ricky

God in Heaven, open your arms,
Richard Nettles is on his way.
He left this earth of hurt and harm,
And will join you soon we pray.

After a long and hard-run race,
He now sits at your feet;
And through your glory and your grace,
You've awakened him from death's sleep.

Although only forty-two
You called our loved one home.
To spend eternity with you,
Never again to be alone.

Dear God, thank you for the good times,
And please let us get over the pain,
And Father, thank you for the sunshine
And help us to understand the rain.

Thank you for the memories,
A better friend we could not have met.
With humbled hearts and bended knees,
Richard Nettles we'll never forget.

Amen

Butchie

Leslie Clifton "Butchie" Mitchell Jr.

Leslie was a husband, father, son, brother, uncle, cousin and friend.

All those who met him wanted to claim him as their kin.

He was a true leader, a soldier, a peer counselor, and a giving veteran;

Having aided service men and retired vets by extending a helping hand.

He believed in duty, and treated everyone with respect.

He was always in control, and always kept himself in check.

He lived his life with compassion and commitment.

His word was his bond, and he said just what he meant!

He loved his wife Sandra, and would give anything for his kids and his grands.

You could tell by the relationship with his siblings that he was a devoted family man.

In his youth, dancing was his passion, which turned into cooking, during his adult years.

He could out step the steppers, and cook better than chefs with successful careers.

He was a flawless dresser, and wore the most unique suites, shoes, and hats.

Fashion just came naturally, and style placed him among elite aristocrats.

From the halls and streets of Cleveland, to the Vegas desert and lights,

He fought the odds, followed his dreams, and rose to prospering heights.

God called him home after seven glorious decades,

Having fulfilled his mission with every debt paid.

God bless this Believer, now among Your best.

Bless the soul of Butchie, and may he forever rest.

You have a place in heaven at the right of God's sacred chair.

Hold tight, don't fret, soon we'll see you there.

Soon I'll see you there!

Aunt Mae

Only two days after Easter,
God called home Aunt Mae.

But we know she died
And was resurrected the same day.

Two birthdays shy of one hundred years,
A glorious long life she lived down here.

Aunt Mae spent her earthly days
Praying for all of us who passed her way.

She prayed for the weak, the down-and-out,
The sick and shut-in, and those in doubt.

She prayed for soldiers like her son-in-law, Butchie,
And first responders, old timers, and rookies.

And for her grandkids like Yarbrough and LaNita,
And her girls; Nadine, Sandra, Pat, Bernice, and Lena.

She worshiped God and was a nurturing soul.
Making it to heaven was her ultimate goal.

A long caring life Aunt Mae lived,
With a heart of gold, and lots of love to give.

And we will tell her story, and sometimes laugh and cry.
But we'll understand things better, bye and bye.

That glorious morning has come,
Now that her earthly days are done.

Pain and suffering will be no more.
She's made it peacefully to Heaven's door.

No more misery. No more sorrow or sadness;
Only dwelling in Jesus' bliss with joy and gladness!

Griffen

A bright candle has, untimely, gone dim.
A loving soul has left us way too soon.
A budding sprout with great promise;
A precious flower, yet to reach full bloom.

There will be many dark days without him,
And our hearts will be overwhelmed and sad;
But there will be joy and happiness on the other side,
So, let us cherish his memories, and be glad.

We believe that prayer is our comfort;
And faith and family are our support.
God will be Griffen's deliverance and salvation,
And our Savior, in this time of sorrow and hurt.

Knowing that he has joined Heaven's band of Angels,
We can rejoice and celebrate his life today;
We ask God for grace and mercy,
And for serenity, and God's blessings, as we pray.

Three

"Tell the truth. Don't blame people!"

George H. W. Bush

In Time, Truth Will Prevail

Time can't wait

And truth is never late.

It may be misled, misinformed, and detoured by a lie.

In darkness, deceit and deception will dissipate

And disappear, and the truth will emerge

With the power to correct and eradicate.

In time truth will prevail,

And the false will forever fail.

Be patient; pause.

And in time, the truth will replace

All deception, and the lie will be erased.

Mendacities will forever be erased!

I Saw the Light

I saw the Light!

And, goodness gracious,

What a spectacular sight;

To see His glory and all its might.

To tell the story

Of the world-saving fight,

And of the truth

That walked this earth

With love;

Without malice or spite.

Just 48 Hours

Just 48 hours to unravel the crime.

Thirty-six hours; don't have much time.

Kidnapping, murder, the loss of life,

The evidence points to the victim's wife.

He was found cut with multiple stabbings.

A crime of passion; throat slashing.

One minute left; she confessed just in time.

Case closed. We solved the crime!

The Real Olympics (1976)

Let me take you to The Real Olympics (1976).

Africa!

Where real life Olympians

Run jump, and vault (triathlons) to flee the dangerous wild.

Where the natives throw spears (javelins) and stones (shot put)

And shoot bows (archery) to secure food and protect the team (tribe).

Not just for the thrill

to kill

but to survive the jungle's ills.

Let me take you to the real Olympics (1976).

Where warriors swim with unmeasured speed

To escape crocodiles and massive beast.

Yet sprint away from stampedes

Only to turn and run-down game

So that the tribe (families) can eat.

Let me take you to the real Olympics (1976).

Where the hunted ward off predators (competitors) to exist (live) another day.

Where survival is every minute and every hour, not even four years.

Where the fittest is for living, not for medals, trophies, and fur.

Let me take you to the real Olympics (1976).

Africa!

Still Here

It's my ticker.
I keep getting sicker!
Passage blocked; arteries getting thicker.
Need a care taker;
Not a heart breaker,
Booty shaker,
Money taker,
Love faker!

Don't need another heart attack.
Next time may not make it back,
(and that's a fact, Jack!)

No heart pitter- patter.
You think my love doesn't matter!
You caused my heart to flat-line for the last time;
No fault; no crime!
I'm going to protect it from your kind.

Go mess up somebody other than me.
Be gone, and set me free!
A new life; a new reality! Fiddle-faddle, riddle-rattle;
Give me the paddles!

CLEAR!
I'm still here!

Haiku

You
can't
take
away
my
pain
and
neither
can
you
destroy
my God's joy!

FOUR

"We've got to see the truth!" First Lady Michelle Obama

It is Us

Altruism doesn't allow us to be selfish,

For it is the exact interaction with all things that exists;

It is the true principal and moral practice that makes us conscience,

free thinking,

and giving human beings;

It is the core of our moral, spiritual, and communal existence.

It is what differentiates humans from all other forms of life.

Altruism is selflessness: no concern for self,

but concern and compassion for everyone

and everything outside of one's personal aura.

Truth is the binder that allows altruism to exist.

It is also the radiant: the infectious component that permeates

in and about all that seek and speak the truth.

Humanitarianism and kindness are the product

and bi-product of altruism.

It lives and breathes and can be contagious.

It is us!

These Formative Years

My Mom taught me how to play marbles;
My Dad, how to build and fly a kite.
My Grandfather taught me how to ride,
And bought me a brand-new bike.

My Grandmother taught me the meaning of work,
And how to make a living.
She also taught me the importance of church,
And the blessings that come from giving.

Watching my Mom, I learned to cook,
And observing Dad, I learned to use my hands.
They nurtured and protected me,
molding this child into a man.

They explained that family comes first,
And the importance of a kiss and a hug.
They instilled in me, "Do what is right.",
And taught me to love and be loved.

I was taught and learned so much
During these formative years.
It set the tone for my future,
And conquered all my fears.

My family pushed me to get an education,
Not knowing how the fees would be paid.
They sacrificed and encouraged me,
And a man of character was made.

Pick-up Sticks

One. Two. Three.

What I recover belongs to me.

Four. Five. Six.

Pick up sticks.

Seven. Eight. Nine.

What I retrieve is mine.

Most points win, according to color.

Orange. Red. Yellow. Blue. Green is the other.

Ten. Eleven. Twelve.

I win. Ring the bell.

Thirteen. Fourteen. Fifteen.

It's a new game. Time to get competitive and mean!

Marbles

To start, lag to the line.
The closest wins.
If there's a tie,
You do it again.

Put your marbles in the **Pot,**
Which is a **Circle** drawn round.
Then take your shot,
with knuckles on the ground.

You can call "knuck's up",
But it's a risk.
With your hand off the ground,
It's easier to miss.

To fill the **Ring,**
Each player puts in ten.
When a marble is knocked out,
You get to shoot again!

All that's expelled
Now belong to you!
It's not gambling.
It's the Marble Golden Rule.

When you miss,
It's the next players turn.
The risk of losing all your marbles
 Is the lesson you will learn.

After your chance,
leave your shooter where it lay.
If knocked out,
Losing the **Pie** is the price you'll pay.

Now you know enough
To lose your marbles and the game.
But with practice you'll succeed,
And file a winning claim.

Pop Goes the Weasel

Pop goes the weasel!

Building blocks,
Goldie Locks,
Measles, Mumps, and Chicken Pocks.

Pop goes the weasel!

A squirrel and moose,
Mother Goose,
And Doctor Seuss.

Pop goes the weasel!

Jump rope, hop scotch,
Pass the potato while it's hot.
It comes to you, and it stops!

Pop goes the weasel!

Chinese Checkers and chess.

Did you pass the test?

Winning is success!

Pop goes the weasel!

The games we play.

The things we say.

Take time to pray!

Before, pop goes the weasel!

What a Meal, What a Meal

Seafood platter with steamed crab, shrimp and fish;

Cole slaw and hush puppies together make a satisfying dish.

Give me southern Fried Chicken wings

With the best crispy onion rings;

Or maybe a prime, grilled medium rare steak,

Or a seasoned beef Wellington freshly baked.

I forgot about pork ribs and chops from BBQ fame,

Cooked to perfection over an open flame.

Potato salad, beans, corn, coleslaw or fries;

It really doesn't matter what's plated as sides.

For dessert, we'll have a freshly prepared cake or pie,

With a scoop of vanilla ice cream on top or on the side.

The best of the best! What a meal! What a meal!

Whatever your fancy; fried, baked, steamed, or grilled.

Chew the Peg (Mumbley-Peg)

Chew the peg!
Underneath the weeping willow tree.
Chew the peg!
Better you than me.

Flip the knife from each finger,
Knuckles and fist.
If you're successful,
Move to the wrist.

Then toss from your elbow,
Shoulder, and knee.
Whatever I do,
Next in turn, follow's my lead.

Loser: With your teeth,
Pull it out of the ground,
Just like a chipmunk
Or bone-digging hound.

If the knife doesn't stick,
You'll have dirt in your mouth
Like ducks in the winter,
Heading for South.

Chew the peg!
Chew the peg!
Out of the dirt
Comes the wooden peg!

Five

"We need to write now,

Write well;

Tell the truth

In all its messy

Complexity."

Jennifer Egan, President of PEN America, a Pulitzer Prize winning author,

and author of the novel, **Manhattan Beach**.

Church Bells Ring, How Sweet the Sound

Church bells ring, how sweet the sound
On Sunday mornings, all over town.

It was Grace AME that blessed us with bells,
Across the street.
Sometimes down, living in defeat,
The joy of chimes helped make life complete.

Sound me the way,
For my vision is in disarray;
Blinded by living,
Disappointed in my giving.

No return on loving.
The dividend has been nothing.
Tired of losing.
Drowned by boozing!
Constantly abusing,
All by my own choosing.

Stop the sideshow
And the merry-go-round.
Replace with truth.
Void of jackals, jokers , and clowns.

Not the Shakers, but the Shook

Gerald Tinker was the fastest man I ever saw run a post.

Lynn Turner could handle a sword better than Aramis or Athos.

I saw **Curly Neal** make a basketball disappear,

And his coach, **Tex Harrison** made the Globetrotters a lifelong career.

Tiger Woods could have been out-played by **Fritz Greer**.

Dylan Smith could throw a baseball faster than all his peers.

And **Jamal Spells** is the best young swimmer that I've ever known,

He is fully committed and disciplined like Olympic superstar, **Simone**.

Cheryl Lynn has more maneuvering skills, ability, and heart,

Than race car drivers, **A. J. Foyt** or **Dale Earnhardt**.

Shela Dawn could fake, dribble, and shoot

Better than **Tina Thompson** or **Cheryl Swoopes**.

Sports is all about who gets the break,

And not about, who has what it really takes.

Champions and heroes are often overlooked,

And neighborhood-Joes are not the takers, but the took!

They're unnoticed for being the movers and shakers,

And ignored, discarded, and are destined to be the shook.

Nothing to Show

Sitting on the side of the bed,
Bowed head,
With a cigarette in his hand.

A bowed head.
Nothing said;
The image of a broken man.

Parked in deep thought.
Life's fight has been fought,
Having done all, he can.

Nothing to show.
Time has taken its toll;
Just a tired face and withered hands.

Another 24 hours,
Nothing new in store;
Just another day of being broke and poor.

The same old grind.
Doing my time
Another day, if I can;

Living off the boss's land.

Win, Place, or Show

The seventh race, and another thirty-dollar bet.
Been here all day, and I haven't won nothing yet!

Already two hundred and 10 dollars in the hole.
I guess it's definitely time to slow my roll.

Should I quit now, with absolutely nothing to show,
Or should I stay and play, or call it a day and go?

"Go home you fool while you still have some cash.
Another few bets, and you'll be out on your ass!"

I'll bet the next race; win, place, or show.
If I don't win and cash in, then I'll go.

My three picks, any way or in-a-row.
They're winners, all; tic-tac-toe!

Now nothing left; broke and busted.
Angry! Mad at myself, and totally disgusted.

Again, there will be words. She won't understand.
She'll cuss and fuss, and say that I'm an unfit man.

I know all and everything that's in store,
Because this scenario has happened before.

I might as well go stay with my cousin, Tyrone.
Lord knows, without the rent, would be stupid to go home!

SIX

"And one of the most important ingredients in a relationship of trust is that we must speak the truth."

Kamala Harris, United States Senator and Author of, ***The Truth we Hold***.

I Got it Right

I decided not to wait for anyone,

And started my journey alone.

In search of a new place;

A place I could call my own.

I headed for the mountains,

In hope of settling there.

But all I found

Were angry people full of hatred and despair.

I turned around,

And headed down

To explore another unknown.

And found myself in a horrible place,

Where hope is never grown.

I turned again, and headed west,

And discovered nothing but dry land.

Here nothing could grow;

Not even cactus, in dehydrated sand.

I then turned east, and to my surprise,

There was light, beauty, and love;

Just the kind of place I think we'll find above.

The question appeared in my mind,

"Should I go back for those I left behind?"

I concluded,

"It's time to forget the past,

And look only to my future!

Following my new path,

Avoiding any and all detours.

There was this illustrious light!

I looked around;

All was well.

This time I know

I got it right.

It's Spring

Looking out of the window, seeing all that is.
Recognizing all creation that's masterfully His,
I know it's Spring!

The blooming flowers
And budding trees.
Green everywhere, from grass to leaves.

Bees are buzzing and birds are singing!
As I view the world,
I know it's Spring.

He died
To save this world from sin.
Now, life renews itself
And never ends.

It's Spring. It's Spring!

Plants and flowers rejuvenate,
Mammals cohabitate,
And fish and fowl procreate,
Because…
It's Spring!

I Killed a Man!

I killed a man

With a rusted paint can.

He grabbed me from behind.

In fear, I lost my mind.

My heart began to pound.

We fell to the ground.

It was dark. Couldn't see.

I felt the can lying beside of me.

I swung it, just one time,

To free me from this crime.

I had to take a stance,

Or be a victim of circumstance.

It wasn't a part of the plan

For me to kill this man.

I just wanted to get away,

And not become his prey.

A bad dream! A bad dream!

What does it mean?

Just the Basics

My Mother believed in the simple things.

No fancy cars or expensive rings.

No lavish meals, with pricey drinks,

or outrageous trips and coats of mink.

Just old-fashioned caring, and the meeting of one's needs;

Compassion for others and doing good deeds.

Just the basics; without the frills.

Life's rewards come from giving, not short-term thrills.

I Could Not Catch Up to Life

I could not catch up to life,

And it would not slow down for me.

So I considered the sacrifice of trading

Living for the right to be free.

Erase the thought of suicide,

And understand that even in darkness,

You cannot hide.

Face your fears and life's uncertainty,

With the promise of light and immortality.

The sun will rise in the East, and as always,

Darkness will surrender and cease.

Life is strange and always complicated.

But by following the light,

It can be emancipated.

Light provides the promise of an eternal home.

And freedom will conquer darkness

And the infinite unknown.

SEVEN

" 'Rotten wood cannot be carved.' I once laughed at that expression. But that was before I lived long enough to see its truth."

Patti LaBelle author of *Patti's Pearls*, page 35, paragraph 2 .

I Am Privileged

I am privileged;

Not because I was born with a silver spoon in my mouth;

Not because my ancestors controlled the south,

But because I have been anointed

And appointed.

No riches, silver, and gold;

No expensive artifacts being traded, or slaves being bought and sold.

I've been blessed with considerable means, yet

Not in ornate objects or material things.

I am adored by a higher power,

Who sits in the tower,

And decides who is the hero

And who is the coward.

I am the conqueror.

And I've been elected, elicited, and uplifted by an appointment to a tumultuous place.

A place of mercy and grace;

A place of forgiving and living,

Of fortitude, without fear,

Or shivering,

Or wavering.

I am here to build on the promise,

And to neutralize conflict and opposition. I will not yield.

There is no appeal!

Summer Days

Summer days;

Go out to play.

Sleep until noon.

Up, not too soon!

Daily chores,

The only bore.

Outdoor adventures,

Fun without censures.

No school, just fun

In the hot blazing sun.

Can't bare the heat;

Nothing on your feet!

In the shade, we sat,

Too hot with sweat.

Playing Old Maid,

While sipping Kool-Aid.

Skimming stones;

Ice cream cones,

Popsicle,

And big dill pickles.

Peanuts and cracker jacks,

Red hots and candy wax.

Bazooka bubble-gum,

And mouth-watering Dum-Dums.

Orange Crush, red pop,

Yoyo's, and spinning tops.

Catching tadpoles.

Fishing without poles.

Marbles in a pot.

Homemade slingshots.

Lightning bugs

And nighttime slugs;

Summer days, summer time,

Those summer days were all mine!

Sunday Morning Prayer

Thank you for such a beautiful day,

And thank you for all you have on display.

Thanks for the flowers and the trees,

And all the things you allow me to see.

Thank you for sunshine and fresh air,

The freedom of thought, and the ability to care.

Thanks for waking me in my right mind,

And giving the strength to leave yesterday behind.

Thanks for helping me get out of bed,

And for knowing to follow you wherever I'm led.

Come into my heart and make me whole,

With a new spirit and cleansed soul.

Guide me through the maze, and keep me safe.

Light my path with your mercy and grace.

Let me face the future with strength and might,

Always keeping your glory within my sight.

Bedtime Baby Rhyme

Mommy and Daddy want you to know

That Mommy and Daddy love you so.

There's nothing anyone can do

To change their unconditional love for you!

So good night.

Be blessed.

Sleep tight

And rest.

Mommy and Daddy love you,

And think you're the best!

EIGHT

Sanctify them by your truth. Your word is truth.

John 17:17, Gideon's New Testament

I'm Tired of That Same Old Grind

I'm tired of that same old grind.

Seems like I'm wasting my time.

I Think it's all by design.

I'm about to lose my mind.

You need to realize

That there's no need for lies,

Or made up stories and alibis.

Because we know the truth never dies.

Truth never dies!

Granny, 100 Years Old

Since your birth in Nineteen Eighteen,
You've come a very long way.
You are forever engaged in the present,
But fully remember the old days.

You have lived to be 100 years old,
And are still in your right mind;
You can say and do what you want
Because you've beat Father Time.

You can fuss when you want,
Even rant and rave,
And demand undivided attention
For the hardship and sacrifice made.

You deserve to have an attitude,
And proclaim right when you're wrong.
You can always blame it on your old age,
And the life you've lived so long.

Although hard of hearing,
And your eyes aren't that great,
You can listen to jazz, watch TV,
And sleep until it's late.

You've been blessed with longevity,
With wisdom greater than we know;
And been given a loving spirit,
That tenderly continues to grow.

You read your Bible, and trust its word,
Both the Old and New Testaments.
You share your knowledge and your faith,
And your days are productively spent.

You will remain an inspiration for others,
With all that your life has been.
May God continue to reward you
Until your eternal life begins.

The Black Poets' Legacy

I knew Gwendolyn brooks.

She gave me her private phone number

And an autographed book.

It was titled "Riot",

And for a dollar,

She let me buy it.

I was so glad,

Because one dollar is all I had.

l didn't know Langston Hughes,

But I understand a festering sore;

Being poor,

Being used

And abused.

Like Mya Angelou,

I too know why caged birds sing,

And what understanding

And wisdom bring.

Nikki Giovanni said it best
When she wrote about inspiration,
Dreams,
And life's unrest.

Poetess Phillis Weatley proceeded us all
With writings of morality
And Religion.
As America's first black published poet,
She had a gift and an anointed vision.

Lastly, l speak of Tupac
And the new poetry we all heard.
Lyrics conceived in modern oppression,
Known as hip hop
And rap;
The new spoken word!

So, may we learn from the genius of those that proceeded us,
By inspiring the next generation, as an obligation and a must.
They all left a poetic history for us to read,
And laid the foundation for future Black poets to succeed.

The Black Poets' Legacy.

To Rewrite History

To rewrite History,

All one must do is

Outlive your peers!

Then,

There's no one

To dispute your recollection!

Not Done Yet

Lots of living and I'm not done yet,
Although life's end is nearing,
There are no regrets.
I have had nine lives,
And with grace I survived.
I suffered;
Lost time
And my mind,
Yet through mercy,
I recovered.
I am blessed and anointed;
Here to tell the story of the Savior
And being saved.
I'm a living witness,
From He who sent us.
My life has been preserved
To share with you this truth
And His word.
I am blessed and anointed,
And you are too!
So, don't ignore truth.
You are sanctified by truth.
Separate.
Excavate.
Emancipate!

NINE

"A lie can go halfway around the world before the truth can put on its pants!"

Mark Twain

A Place for All

I don't feel sorry for myself.

l feel sad for everyone else:

The down and out,

All those in doubt,

The misused and abused,

Those defeated and those who lose.

I feel sorry for those who are frozen in a trance,

And for those stifled by circumstance.

All I ask is for an equal playing field,

A solid foundation from whence all can build,

A place of giving and caring,

A place of community and sharing,

A place without hate and unbearable stress,

A place of love and happiness,

A place where everyone takes a stance,

To assure that all have a fighting chance!

Truth Never Dies

I saw it,

But I said and did nothing.

I heard it,

But I lent a deaf ear.

I committed the crime,

But blamed it on another.

I told a straight up lie,

And swore, on the name of my Mother.

I ran away when others stayed.

I hid because I was so afraid.

I tried to bury the truth,

And conceal my identity with a mask.

In time, I learned,

"Truth never dies and will forever last."

MY MIND

Yes, I walk with a cane,

But there's nothing wrong with my brain!

I get confused sometimes,

But I'm far from losing my mind.

My nerves are painfully bad,

And my mobility is not what I once had.

My mind is sound and sharp,

And I still feel love in my heart.

I am physically weak,

But my intelligence is at its peak.

Don't count me out.

I will surpass all your doubts!

The Parade

The parade

Is a masquerade;

Hidden faces and hidden deed,

Cover up, sabotage,

And open wounds that bleed.

Don't believe the hype

And false fanfare.

Seek the truth!

Beneath all the many layers.. care!

Don't follow the drum major

Or the beat of the band.

Follow your conscience,

And make a lasting stand.

Make your own music and rhyme.

Do it now.. double time!

Be new! Be true!

Be the beginning,

And the responsible you!

TEN

"We hold these truths to be self-evident, that all men are created equal, that they are endowed by their Creator with certain unalienable Rights, that among these are Life, Liberty and the pursuit of Happiness."

Thomas Jefferson, Declaration of Independence

Blessings

Bless somebody today!
Bless them and give them grace.

Be merciful and forgiving.
Be caring and lift up their living.

Encourage their spirit.
Inspire them to never quit!

Treat them as if they were new,
With all that is good, all that is true.

Bless them, don't judge.
And blessings will be multiplied,
And be bestowed upon you!

My 1958 Olds

Down the dirt road and up the hill

In my Rocket 88 Oldsmobile.

Everybody looking, checking it out.

Black on black, 3-inch white wall, rolling with clout!

Yes, it's a Sedan, two door,

With headlights of four,

Covered with chrome bumpers, and aluminum trim,

And tail gas tank is in the rear; brake light fin.

A 1958, with the engine a 231,

Fast and powerful, second to none.

Over 45 years she's been my best friend.

I will continue to pamper her around every bend!

Four/forty; windows down, catching the breeze!

I thank old Mr. Shelly for selling her to me.

The Lie

It's called perjury, if you lie on the stand.

It's called obstruction, if you lie to the Man.

It's called dishonesty, if you lie to your boss,

Infidelity, if you cheat on your spouse, and lines are crossed.

For most, truth comes naturally;

But for some lying emanates so easily.

There's no hiding place for Liars.

They will be exposed by the town criers.

Pilish

3.1415926535

Joy!

I love a cream milkshake at sunset.

Enjoy and smile!

"Tell the Truth!"
- Marvin M. Young VIII

Sheldon D. Stovall

Sheldon D. Stovall is a native of Ohio, who has 35 years of experience working with non-profit organizations. Mr. Stovall, now retired, has a Bachelor of Arts degree in English from Kent State University and a Master's degree in Public Administration from Texas Southern University. He served as the YMCA of Greater Houston Poet Laureate for over thirteen years. He also designed the YMCA of the USA National Diversity lapel pin.

He is a former member of the Columbus, Ohio Mental Health Board, and a former adjunct professor for Springfield College, a Certified Mindful Coach, a certified Public Notary, and a Human Services-Board Certified Practitioner (HS-BCP), for the State of Texas.

Professor Stovall is community minded and is a member of many organizations that are service oriented. He has been a Loaned Executive to the United Way, a member of the YMCA of the USA Diversity Initiative Advisory Team (D.I.A.T.), has served on the University of Houston American Humanistic Advisory Board and the Board of the Living Bank.

He is a member of the Association of YMCA Retirees (AYR), the NAACP, Alpha Phi Alpha Fraternity, Inc., Leadership Houston Class XV, the Society for Human Resources Management, and a 32nd Degree Mason. He has received numerous prestigious awards and recognition. Sheldon and his wife of 45 years, Cheryl, have two adult children. Sheldon and Cheryl reside in Houston, Texas.